D0111995

PROJECT FUN-WAY

Starring

RUSSELL FERGUSON

Written by Ellie O'Ryan

Little, Brown and Company
New York Boston

Little, Brown and Company

Hachette Book Group
1290 Avenue of the Americas, New York, NY 10104
Visit us at lb-kids.com

Little, Brown and Company is a division of Hachette Book Group, Inc. The Little, Brown name and logo are trademarks of Hachette Book Group, Inc.

First Edition: October 2015

ISBN 978-0-316-30138-1

10 9 8 7 6 5 4 3 2 1

RRD-C

Printed in the United States of America

For Finley Rae Hahn

CONTENTS

Chapter 1

Bzzz. Bzzz. Bzzz.

Blythe Baxter pulled the pillow over her head.

Bzzz. Bzzz. Bzzz.

What *was* that buzzing noise?

Bzzz. Bzzz. Bzzz.

It wasn't the alarm clock. Tomorrow was

Saturday; Blythe could sleep in as late as she wanted.

So what was it?

Eventually, Blythe couldn't ignore the noise any longer. She sat up in bed, rubbed her eyes, and turned on the light. That's when Blythe noticed her cell phone buzzing like crazy as it vibrated across her bedside table. The clock on her desk read 2:53 AM.

Who's calling me in the middle of the night? Blythe wondered sleepily as she reached for the phone. She pressed the answer button and mumbled, "Hello?"

"*Blythe*, darling, how *are* you?"

Blythe sat up straighter, completely wide awake. There was no mistaking that voice— it was the one and only Mona Autumn, publisher of the world-famous fashion magazine *Tres Blasé*. Mona was a glittering star in the fashion world, and Blythe had been in awe of her ever since Blythe sketched her very first fashion design.

Fashion wasn't Blythe's only passion, though. She also loved pets—all pets. And through the Littlest Pet Shop, Blythe was lucky enough to be able to combine both of her passions! Not only were Blythe's adorable and glamorous pet fashions for sale at the Littlest Pet Shop, Blythe also got to hang out with the wonderful pets who attended Day Camp there. The pets were always happy to model Blythe's latest designs, but more importantly, they were her friends.

Everybody knew that Blythe loved fashion, especially designing her own unique outfits. But what people *didn't* know was that Blythe had a top secret ability that she would never, ever reveal to anyone. Blythe could communicate with animals! At first, Blythe was incredibly freaked out by her unusual talent, but as she got used to it, Blythe started to understand just how amazing it was to understand animals, especially her pet friends. Not only could she help them when other people couldn't, but the pets could help Blythe whenever she needed them. She and the pets had had so many amazing adventures together—including a recent trip to the international Pet Fashion Expo, where Blythe and one of her pet pals, Russell the hedgehog, had been photographed for *Tres Blasé*! That was how Blythe had managed to meet someone as important and influential as Mona Autumn.

"I'm calling from Paris with the most fabulous news," Mona said briskly. "Are you sitting down, Blythe? Because you really should be sitting down."

Does lying down count? Blythe wondered. But before she could reply, Mona continued.

"Our latest issue of *Tres Blasé*—yes, that's right, the one with you and your prickly pet—has sold more than half a million copies!"

Blythe gasped. Half a million copies? That news wasn't just fantastic—it was amazing. Astonishing. Unbelievable!

"Half a million copies?" Blythe repeated, still in shock.

"And still selling! We simply can't print them fast enough!" Mona crowed. "Needless to say, *everyone's* thrilled. The fashion industry's thrilled. Our advertisers are thrilled. Even *I'm* thrilled—and I am *very* hard to thrill."

"I'm so—" Blythe started, but once more, Mona kept talking.

"And the public! The public is *beyond* thrilled! What they want, Blythe, is more. More Blythe Style, more fashion hedgehog, more *Tres Blasé*, more, more, more! And do you know what we're going to do?"

This time, Blythe didn't even try to answer.

"We're going to give it to them!" Mona answered her own question. "That's where you come in. We want you and Russell as the headline stars for a very special event being held in Paris in ten days!"

"A fashion show?" Blythe was so excited her voice sounded all squeaky.

"Better," Mona declared. "A fashion show at the first-ever Everyday Hero Awards, right on the runway at the Paris airport!"

Blythe gasped. "Mona, I'm honored," she said.

"Yes, of course you are," Mona replied. "This is big, Blythe. Really big. All eyes will be on you—which is what makes it so wonderful, since that means they'll also be on the everyday heroes who are being honored for their, well, heroics. Heroes get recognition, you get stardom, *Tres Blasé* gets to sell one *million* copies of our next issue. Everybody wins!"

Blythe grabbed her notebook and a pen. "Which fashions should I bring for the show?" she asked.

"Bring? No, no, no—you mean *design*," Mona corrected her. "We want all-new designs debuted here, Blythe. The public demands it. Now, for some direction: I want you to think *daring* and *dramatic* for your designs. Just like the heroes we'll be honoring."

Blythe wasn't sure she'd heard Mona correctly. "I'm sorry—did you say *all-new* designs?" she repeated. "For a show that's in *two weeks*?"

"Not two weeks. Ten days," Mona said. "But there's no need to panic, Blythe. I'm sure you can come up with at least seven new designs by then. After all, you're a *real* designer, aren't you?"

"Um, yes, of course," Blythe said, trying to sound confident. But inside, she was about ten seconds away from panicking! Mona was asking for a lot—especially considering that Blythe was also juggling school and her responsibilities at the Littlest Pet Shop. But Blythe didn't want to let Mona down—or blow this amazing opportunity.

"We're giving you a lot of control, Blythe," Mona told her. "Since you'll be the only designer for this show, you'll get to make all the big decisions—from sets and lights to models—"

Blythe perked up immediately. "You mean I can choose the pet models, all by myself?"

"Exactly," replied Mona.

Blythe wanted to cheer out loud, but instead she did a silent fist pump. Before the photo shoot, Blythe had told her pet pals that they could all be involved—but then Mona changed her mind. That's how Russell had become the star of the photo shoot. The other pets weren't too upset, but Blythe felt bad all the same. She finally had a chance to make it up to them.

"I've got to run, but I'll call back soon

to finalize all the details," Mona continued. "Be ready to *wow* me, Blythe! *Ciao!*"

And just like that, Blythe's phone went silent.

"Bye, Mona," Blythe whispered. She put her phone back on the bedside table but didn't turn off the light. Instead, Blythe reached for her sketchbook and her favorite colored pencils. She had an international fashion show to prepare for—in *only* ten days.

There wasn't a moment to lose!

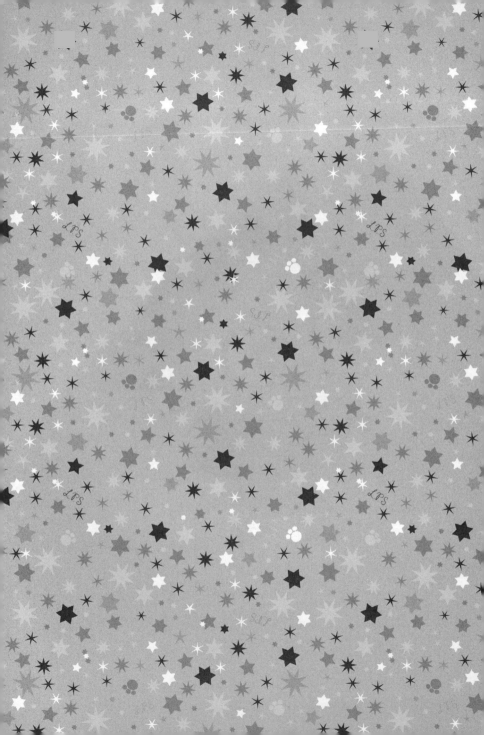

Chapter 2

The next morning, Blythe's dad, Roger, put on his pilot uniform and went to the kitchen to make some coffee before heading to the airport. He was surprised to see that Blythe was already in the kitchen—and from the look of the table, she'd been up for hours! The table was completely covered with pages from Blythe's sketchbook, fabric swatches, and a whole bunch of crumpled-up pieces of paper that were destined for the trash can.

"Whoa! What day is it?" Roger asked, squinting at his watch. "I could've sworn it was Saturday—"

"It *is* Saturday, Dad," Blythe replied. "You are *never* going to believe the phone call I got!" She quickly told him everything.

"I know it's pretty last minute, but can you take the pets and me to Paris in ten days?" Blythe asked. "It's an opportunity of a lifetime, and I'd hate to miss it."

"Miss it? Are you kidding?" Roger exclaimed. "It will be an honor to fly you and the pets to Paris. My daughter's going to be an international fashion superstar! I'll be the proudest dad in the whole wide world!"

"Thank you so much!" Blythe cried as she grinned at her dad. Though she missed him when he had to travel for work, there were a lot of perks to having a pilot for a father. And with the fully equipped Pet Jet at their service, Blythe and her pals from the Littlest Pet Shop could always travel in style—no matter where they needed to go.

Roger checked his watch again. "I don't have to be at the airport for a couple of hours," he said. "How about we go out to breakfast to celebrate? What do you say, Blythe...waffles with extra whipped cream?"

"I wish I could," Blythe replied. "But I've got to get downstairs as soon as Day Camp opens. There's so much work to do, and I can't wait to tell the pets about the trip! I know they'll be so excited—"

Too late Blythe realized what she'd said.

"I mean, *their owners* will be so excited," she quickly corrected herself. Not even Blythe's dad knew that she could communicate with animals. Luckily, though, he didn't seem to notice her slip.

"That's my girl," said Roger. "Always keeping her eyes on the prize!"

Blythe stood up, neatly stacked her sketches, and threw away the crumpled pages. "I guess I'll head downstairs," she said. "Mrs. Twombly should be opening the shop any minute now."

"Sounds great, Blythe," Roger said. "I'm scheduled for a short round-trip flight today, so I'll be back in time for dinner."

"See you then!" Blythe said as she hurried out of the apartment. Blythe loved living in Downtown City. It was such an amazing place, full of energy and excitement.

Of all the amazing things Downtown City offered—from museums and concerts to cafés and parks—Blythe's favorite place in the city was the Littlest Pet Shop. Sometimes she couldn't believe how lucky she was to live right upstairs!

When Blythe arrived at the Littlest Pet Shop, she found the owner, Mrs. Twombly, behind the counter, where she was organizing the jeweled collars by color.

"Good morning, Blythe," Mrs. Twombly said. "You're here early. Is everything okay?"

"Morning, Mrs. Twombly!" Blythe replied. "You'll never guess what happened!"

As Blythe told Mrs. Twombly all about Mona Autumn's phone call, Mrs. Twombly's mouth dropped open. "Oh, Blythe! I'm so happy for you!" she squealed.

"Thanks—I still can't believe it," said

Blythe, shaking her head in amazement. "If you'll excuse me, I need to go see how my *models* are doing today!"

Blythe pushed through the curtain that separated the shop from the Day Camp. Sure enough, all the regulars had arrived. Blythe spotted Penny Ling, the gentle and graceful panda, making a beautiful new ribbon stick for her rhythm dancing. Artistic and mischievous Minka the monkey was splattering paint across a blank canvas to create one of her unique pieces of artwork. Vinnie the gecko and Sunil the mongoose couldn't be more different—Vinnie was extra easygoing, while Sunil was a serious worrywart—but that didn't get in the way of their friendship. They loved hanging out! Meanwhile, reliable Russell the hedgehog and silly Pepper the skunk were playing hide-and-seek.

"Guess what, everybody?" Blythe asked. "Mona Autumn called with big news!"

All the pets stopped what they were doing and turned to Blythe to hear more. One pet in particular—a Cavalier King Charles spaniel named Zoe—pranced right over to Blythe. Zoe had lots of experience in the spotlight. In addition to modeling, Zoe had even starred on the reality show *Terriers and Tiaras*. Walking the runway to model Blythe's fabulous fashions was one of Zoe's favorite things to do...so when Zoe heard the name *Mona Autumn*, she couldn't wait to find out more.

Blythe took a deep breath as the rest of the pets gathered around her. "The latest issue of *Tres Blasé* has had record-breaking sales, so Mona has invited me to do a special fashion show at an awards ceremony... in Paris!"

The pets erupted into such loud applause that Blythe put her hands over her ears, and she started laughing. "Isn't it amazing?" she asked as soon as they quieted down. "And here's the best part—since the show is going to feature my designs exclusively, I get to choose all the models. That means that *all* of you can be in the show! I'm going to ask your owners for permission today!"

"Oh, Blythe, this is like a dream come true!" Zoe cried, fluttering her long eyelashes. "I've always wanted to star in a fashion show in the *fashion capital* of the world!"

Blythe tried to hide her smile. She didn't want any one pet to be the star—she wanted them all to feel equally important as they modeled her designs. "Well, from the way Mona was talking, it sounds like you'll *all* be stars," Blythe explained.

"So when is this show, anyway?" Russell asked.

"Well..." Blythe began, biting her lip a little. "It's in ten days—so we have our work cut out for us. Mona wants me to create all-new designs and be responsible for planning a lot of the other parts of the show, too..."

"Don't you worry, Blythe," Zoe said confidently. "I have complete faith in you!"

"Thanks, Zoe," Blythe said. "I guess I just—"

Bzzzz!

Blythe's phone was buzzing again. "Maybe it's Mona Autumn!" she exclaimed. At the same time, the Littlest Pet Shop phone started ringing, too. *Brrrring!*

"Anyway, I just need to—" Blythe continued as she searched for her phone.

Bzzzz! Brrring!

"—stay—"

Bzzzz! Brrring!

"—focused!" Blythe finished triumphantly as she finally found her phone at the bottom of her bag. "Hello? Oh, hi, Youngmee."

Youngmee Song, one of Blythe's best friends, worked part-time at the Sweet Delights Sweet Shoppe next door.

"Look outside?" Blythe said into her phone, sounding confused. "Why? Is something going on? Oh...okay. Call you right back."

Blythe hung up and turned back to the pets. "Youngmee's being very mysterious," she said. "I guess we'd better go see what's up."

The pets followed Blythe through the Day Camp area to the front of the store, where Mrs. Twombly was frantically trying to handle the phone. The instant she finished one call, the phone started ringing again! Beyond that, though, the store was packed with customers. The Littlest Pet Shop was usually busy catering to animal lovers who lived in Downtown City and visiting tourists, but Blythe couldn't remember a time when so many people had packed into the small shop—not even during the holiday rush.

There was no doubt about it: Something very unusual was happening.

And Blythe and the pets were about to find out what.

Chapter 3

Blythe crossed the shop and opened the door. Her mouth dropped open. The sidewalk in front of the Littlest Pet Shop was crowded with photographers, reporters, and cameramen. There was even a news van parked at the curb!

"What—" Blythe began.

That was when the reporters noticed

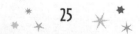

her. "Blythe! Blythe! Blythe!" they cried as they rushed over. "Just a few questions—a quick interview—"

Quick-thinking Minka darted around Blythe and slammed the door shut. Blythe grabbed the remote control from the counter and turned on the TV—just in time to catch a glimpse of herself standing in the doorway of the Littlest Pet Shop as Minka slammed the door!

"That's—here?" Blythe asked in shock. "Happening—now?"

"Shhh! Quiet down!" Vinnie said as the reporter started talking—but to Mrs. Twombly and all the customers, it sounded like an ordinary gecko noise.

"I'm coming to you live from the Littlest Pet Shop right here in Downtown City, where some very big dreams are about to come true!" the reporter said into her microphone. "Blythe Baxter, chief designer of the Blythe Style line of pet fashions, which are sold exclusively here at the Littlest Pet Shop, has been handpicked by fashion pioneer Mona Autumn as the featured designer for an upcoming show in Paris, France!"

Blythe stood in shock as her phone slid from her hand. It clattered to the floor and immediately started buzzing again.

"The Paris offices of *Tres Blasé* have announced that more details about the show will be released soon," the reporter continued breathlessly. "Until then, we suggest you snatch up as many Blythe Style original pet fashions as you can. With Blythe on her way to superstardom, her creations are sure to be in high demand! As you can see, there's such a large crowd inside the Littlest Pet Shop that people have formed a line outside that stretches halfway down the block! There's no doubt about it: Blythe Baxter is the hottest designer in the world—and if you want your pets wearing her looks, the Littlest Pet Shop is the only place to be!"

At that moment, someone in the shop glanced up at the TV just as the news station flashed Blythe's school picture across the screen. The customer's gaze drifted over to Blythe, who was standing beside her. It took a moment for her to make the connection, but suddenly her eyes lit up.

"Blythe?" she shrieked. "Blythe Baxter? *The* Blythe Baxter of Blythe Style? This is such an honor! Can I get your autograph?"

"Me too!" another woman exclaimed. "And one for my daughter? And my niece?

And my next-door neighbor's second cousin?"

"Uh—uh—uh—" Blythe stammered as the crowd surged around her.

Luckily, the pets knew just what to do. They surrounded Blythe and quickly nudged her toward the Day Camp area of the shop, where customers weren't allowed. Once they were all safely in the private area of the store, Blythe breathed a sigh of relief and flopped down in a comfortable chair.

"Thanks, everybody," she said gratefully. "That was..."

"Intense," suggested Sunil.

"Insane," Russell said, shaking his head.

"Incredible!" Zoe added. "Blythe, can you *believe* it? You're an international superstar! We always knew you had the talent... and now the *whole* world knows!"

But instead of rejoicing like Zoe, a worried expression settled over Blythe's face. "It's kind of overwhelming," she confessed. "That crowd out there...all those people acting like I'm a celebrity..."

"Look at it this way," Pepper pointed out. "All those customers mean that Mrs. Twombly is going to sell even more stuff than usual...which means the Littlest Pet Shop will be more successful than ever! All thanks to you!"

Blythe smiled, but the worried look didn't leave her eyes. "It's just a lot of pressure...and stress," she said. "I mean...what if I can't get everything done in time? And I'm not even sure yet what Mona wants me to do for the fashion show itself—besides design and sew all-new outfits. I've never been in charge of a fashion show! I don't even know where to begin!"

Russell and Zoe exchanged a glance. The other pets seemed concerned, too. The last thing they wanted was for Blythe's amazing opportunity to turn into a huge stressor for her!

Russell knew that he had to find a way to reassure Blythe. "You're not alone in this, Blythe!" he told her. "We'll help you every step of the way. Whatever you need—you can count on us."

"Definitely!" added Penny Ling. The rest of the pets nodded.

"You know," Russell began, "I just had an idea. Why don't *we* focus on plans for the fashion show itself... while you focus on the new designs?"

Blythe blinked in surprise. "You'd do that for me?" she asked.

"Of *course* we would," Russell assured her. "Let's face it, Blythe. Mona's asking you to do the impossible—creating all-new designs *and* organizing an entire fashion show in just ten days?"

"Yeah!" Pepper piped up. "That's crazy talk!"

"You'll still be in charge, of course," Russell continued. "I think Mona was right to give you creative control over the whole show. Nobody does fashion like you! But we can do a lot of the planning work for you behind the scenes. You know how much I like organizing things!"

Blythe looked around at the eager faces of all her pet friends. "I don't know what to say," Blythe told them. "This would take away so much stress. It would actually make the fashion show feel like fun again!"

"And it *should* be fun," Russell said firmly. "Don't worry about the runway; focus on the FUN-way! Project FUN-way! So what do you say?"

"Yes—a million times over!" Blythe replied at once. "I can't thank you all enough."

Russell grinned as he whipped out a notebook and pencil. "Let's get started right away!" he announced. "What did you say the feel of the show should be?"

"Daring and dramatic," Blythe said. "The fashion show is part of an awards ceremony for everyday heroes—I bet all the heroes were involved in daring and dramatic rescues or something like that. So it's up to us to make it all fit together."

"Let us worry about that," Russell told her. "Why don't you get to work on your designs, and we'll have a meeting to see what everyone's come up with."

"That sounds perfect," Blythe said. "If you need anything—anything at all—you know where to find me."

With her sketchbook and colored pencils tucked under her arm, Blythe hurried off to the side room where she stored all her sewing supplies. Russell held his arms open wide.

"Pet huddle!" he announced, gesturing for the other Day Campers to come closer. "Blythe needs us more than ever before— and this is our chance to help her out."

"You know you can count on us," Sunil said.

"For starters, I don't think we should

interrupt Blythe for any reason at all," Russell said. "Even though she said we could. It's our job to make her life easier, not harder."

"I agree," Penny Ling said, nodding. "Besides, no matter what comes up, we can handle it."

"That's the right attitude!" Russell said approvingly. "So whatever you need, you should come to me instead."

"I'm so glad you're going to be in charge, Russell," said Minka as she hopped from one foot to the other. "You're the most organized hedgehog I know! I mean, you're the *only* hedgehog I know—but it's, like, really super-duper important that somebody organized take control."

"Me? In charge?" Russell asked in surprise. "No, no—that's not what I meant at all. I was just—"

"But *somebody's* got to be in charge," Pepper interrupted him. "Otherwise, we won't know who's doing what."

"Things could fall through the cracks," Sunil added. "And that would make Blythe more stressed out than ever."

"But—" Russell argued.

"They're right, buddy," Vinnie spoke up. "You're the perfect hedgehog for the job."

There was a pause before Russell spoke. "Well…if you're all sure," he said as he finally gave in. "I'll only be in charge if everybody *wants* me to be in charge. You know what? Let's have a vote! That way, we know it's all fair and square."

The other pets smiled to themselves. Everybody knew that Russell was the obvious choice to be in charge—everybody except Russell himself. But if it would make

Russell feel better to hold a vote, then that's exactly what they would do.

Russell made sure that the tip of his pencil was extra sharp as he wrote everyone's name down in his notebook. Then he cleared his throat. "Everybody who thinks that I should be in charge, please raise your paw," he said in a very serious-sounding voice.

Vinnie stared at his sticky toes. "What if you don't have paws?" he asked.

"Raising your foot will be fine," Russell told him.

In an instant, Minka's, Pepper's, Penny Ling's, Sunil's, and Vinnie's paws shot into the air. Russell blushed with happiness as he made a check mark next to each name. The vote was almost unanimous... *almost.*

Russell's smile faded. "Zoe?" he asked. "Where's Zoe?"

The other pets looked around the room. Somehow, Zoe had slipped away from the group...and no one had noticed.

"Hmm," Russell said. "I guess our first order of business will be...finding Zoe."

"Maybe she's playing hide-and-seek!" Minka exclaimed as she scampered around Day Camp, searching for Zoe under every chair and in every cupboard.

"Oh, Minka! Zoe's not playing hide-and-seek," Pepper said in frustration. "She knows there's way too much work to do for games."

"Hide-and-seek isn't a game!" Minka retorted. "It's very serious business!"

Russell held up his paws. "Let's not argue," he said. "It's pretty clear that Zoe's not in the Day Camp area. Which can only mean..."

As Russell's voice trailed off, everyone looked toward the store section of the Littlest Pet Shop. If Zoe had snuck back there, with all the customers and cameras...

"Uh-oh," Sunil said—which was exactly what everybody else was thinking.

"Remember, we can't bother Blythe," Russell told his friends. He took a deep breath. "You stay here. I'm going in."

"Good luck, boss," Vinnie said as he patted Russell on the back.

"You can do it!" added Penny Ling.

Russell crept toward the store, wondering what he'd find there. An out-of-control crowd? A frenzied pack of reporters? Mrs. Twombly with a phone stuck to each ear?

Nothing could have prepared him for the reality: Zoe was strutting back and forth on the counter, modeling Blythe's creations in an impromptu fashion show while all the photographers took pictures of her! Even though Mrs. Twombly was working furiously at the cash register to ring up every purchase, the line of customers stretched all the way out the door.

A wide grin crossed Russell's face as he shook his head. He should've known Zoe would do something like this. The call of the cameras and the lure of the spotlight were just too tempting for her to resist. But how would he ever persuade her to come back to Day Camp?

Then Russell stopped. *Maybe I* don't *have to bring Zoe back with me,* he thought. *She's plenty happy right where she is . . . and her modeling is boosting sales . . .* and *she's keeping the photographers busy, which means they're not bugging Blythe. Yes! This is working out just fine.*

With all the commotion, none of the customers had noticed the little hedgehog who'd appeared—then disappeared—so suddenly. But Russell was beaming as he joined the rest of the pets at Day Camp. He couldn't have been more pleased with his first decision as leader. If everything else went this smoothly, Russell was confident that pulling off the fashion show would be a piece of cake!

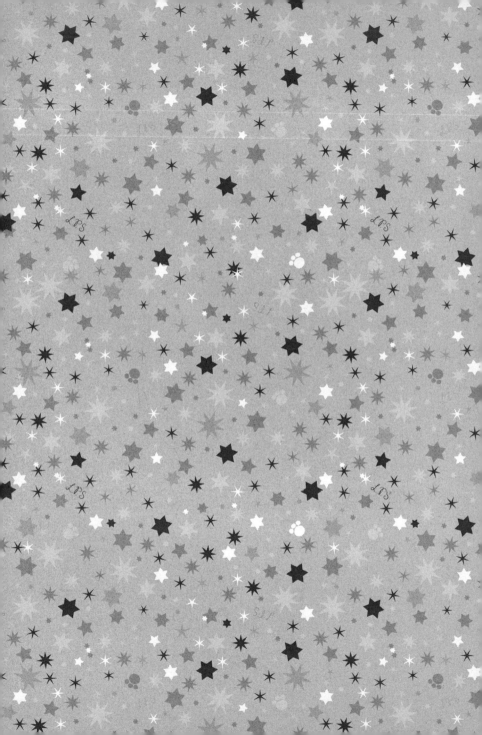

Chapter 4

Over the next few days, Russell and the other pets split up so they could focus on brainstorming unique ideas to make the fashion show feel "daring and dramatic." Russell worked nonstop to come up with brilliant ideas for Project FUN-way. Eventually, his notebook was full of them—a huge white tent, extra-bright clear lightbulbs, silver sawhorses. *This might actually work,* Russell thought excitedly as he reviewed his lists. *By keeping everything in the background as plain as possible, with lots of white and silver, Blythe's fashions will really pop!*

"Russell! I've had the absolute best idea for the fashion show!" Zoe gushed as she hurried up to him. "I was thinking...how can we make a fashion show even *more* dramatic and exciting? And you know what I thought of? Circuses!"

Russell's face scrunched up in confusion. "Circuses?" he repeated. *What do circuses have to do with everyday heroes?* he wondered.

"Yes, exactly!" Zoe said. "Lion tamers... trapeze artists...high-wire acts...you just don't get more dramatic than that!"

"I...guess not," Russell said. He didn't

want to hurt Zoe's feelings. But the truth was, Russell thought her idea was all wrong!

Zoe clapped her paws together. "Oh, I just *knew* you'd agree!" she cried. "Now, here's what we'll need—better grab your notebook, Russell, you'll want to write this down."

Slowly, Russell reached for his notebook. *I guess it wouldn't hurt to write it down,* he thought. *It will make Zoe feel like she's an important part of our team. And I'll just make sure that my ideas are the ones we use in the show, because they are better for showcasing Blythe's fashions.*

"For starters, we need giant spotlights in all colors," Zoe said excitedly. "And... some kind of fancy tinsel curtain for the backdrop. You know, something shiny and sparkly. And you know what would be *really* great?"

"What?" Russell asked hesitantly as he tucked his pencil behind his ear. He didn't know how much more "greatness" he could handle!

"We could hire trapeze artists to perform in the air while we're all walking the runway!" Zoe exclaimed. "You just don't get more *dramatic* than that!"

"Right. Trapeze artists," Russell said— but this time, he didn't even write it down.

"Aren't you going to add it to the list?" she asked.

"Oh. Yeah. Sure, I guess," Russell said.

Minka scampered over to them. "Hey! What are you guys doing?" she asked.

"I was just telling Russell all about my vision for Blythe's fashion show," Zoe told her.

"Ooh, you know what? I had an idea for the show, too!" Minka exclaimed.

Russell brightened a little. Everyone knew that Minka was incredibly artistic. Her flash of inspiration might be the perfect way to make the fashion show unforgettable. "What's your idea, Minka?" Russell asked as he reached for his pencil again.

"Fireballs!" Minka announced.

"Fireballs?" Russell and Zoe repeated in disbelief. Russell snuck a glance at Zoe out of the corner of his eye. He was relieved to see that she looked as shocked as he felt. Of course, Russell wasn't sure why he was so surprised. Minka wasn't just imaginative and artistic. Sometimes she was entirely over the top, too!

"You know. Special effects. Pyro-what's-it-called," Minka continued.

"Pyrotechnics," Russell corrected her. But before he could tell Minka that there would be absolutely *no* fireballs at the fashion show, Zoe started to speak.

"Minka, you're a genius!" she declared.

Russell shook his head. *Did I hear Zoe correctly?* he wondered. *Surely she didn't just say that Minka's—*

"An absolute *genius!*" Zoe continued. "Fireballs are perfect. Talk about danger! Real fire and flames lighting up the runway! In fact—"

"Whoa, whoa, whoa," Russell interrupted as he held up his paws. "Nope. No way. No how. We can't have *fireballs* at the show! That's way too dangerous!"

Minka scrunched up her face. "But, Russell, the theme of the show is danger," she pointed out. "Dangerous and dramatic. And anyway, it's just a special effect. It's not like we're going to start a bonfire onstage or anything. Though, on second thought..."

"No!" Russell yelped. "First, it's *daring* and dramatic. Not *dangerous* and dramatic. And second—no fire at all!"

"But the pyrotechnics would be controlled by a trained professional," Zoe said reassuringly. "And I know for a fact that Blythe has been working on a firefighter-inspired fashion design. Not to mention, fire fits in *perfectly* with my circus theme!"

Minka clapped her hands together. "So you're thinking there could be, like, a fire-eater?"

Russell was getting flustered. He knew he had to put a stop to this crazy idea before it went any further. He took a deep breath and said, as calmly as he could, "I agree that it *sounds* very exciting and dramatic. But I'm in charge, and I take that very seriously. And the truth is, real fire is just too dangerous for my fashion show."

"*Your* fashion show?" Zoe repeated, raising an eyebrow. "I thought it was *Blythe's* fashion show."

Every last one of Russell's prickly spines bristled. "Yes, and everyone voted for *me* to be in charge," he snapped. "And I say *no fire!*"

Minka and Zoe exchanged a worried look.

"But Blythe would still want to hear all our ideas," Minka pointed out.

"I agree," Zoe said. "Add Minka's idea to

the list. If Blythe doesn't want to do it, then that's her decision. But she should at least get to hear all the ideas. That's only fair."

Russell realized that Zoe and Minka weren't going to give up—no matter what he said. "Oh, all right," he said, sounding annoyed. "I'll add fireballs to the list. But don't say I didn't warn you if Blythe hates your idea."

Zoe and Minka watched as Russell scribbled the word *fireballs* on the list. "Thanks, Russell," Minka said in a quiet voice. She almost sounded sad. "I...only wanted to help. It...seemed like a good idea."

Then Russell had a good idea of his own. "You know, Minka, if you *really* want to help—help Blythe!" he suggested.

Minka looked surprised. "Help Blythe?

How?" she asked. "I thought I was helping by staying out of her way. Besides, I don't even know how to use a sewing machine!"

"I've got a better idea," Russell said importantly. "Minka, from now on, it's your job to be at Blythe's beck and call! It's up to you to figure out what Blythe needs—even before she knows she needs it!"

Minka looked baffled. "How in the world am I supposed to do that?" she asked.

"Never leave her side," Russell ordered. "If she takes her last sip of water, you get her a new water bottle before she has a chance to ask for one. If she drops a needle, you grab it before it even hits the floor. If she finishes her snack—"

"Get her another one," Minka finished for him.

"Yes! That's exactly it!" Russell exclaimed.

"You know, it's a big job. And an important one. So, Zoe, you'd better help, too."

"Well, sure, I guess," Zoe replied. "I'd do anything for Blythe."

"Of course you would," Russell said with a smile. "You know, she might need something right now—and there's no one there to help her!"

"I guess we'd better hurry, then!" Minka said.

As Minka and Zoe hurried off to Blythe's sewing room at the back of the shop, Russell sighed with relief. *I'm so glad I found a good job for them*, he thought. *Now I can get back to plans for Project FUN-way without any more silly interruptions.*

Even as the thought crossed his mind, Russell's spines prickled a little. In his heart, he knew that Zoe and Minka weren't silly interruptions. They were some of his very best friends. But Russell pushed the thought from his mind. Right now, he had to focus on Project FUN-way.

No matter what.

Chapter 5

Blythe was so busy sewing that she completely missed the change in Russell. The pets, however, were not so lucky. No one knew what to do about the new-and-definitely-*not*-improved Russell, but all the pets agreed that they couldn't bother Blythe about it—not when she had so much work to do.

When Blythe finally sewed the last stitch on the last outfit, the sudden silence of her sewing machine filled the entire Day Camp. The pets had gotten so used to hearing it that the quiet seemed much louder than usual.

"I'm done," Blythe said, looking tired but happy. "I just finished the very last outfit for the fashion show!"

A tremendous cheer arose from all the pets as they swarmed around Blythe to congratulate her.

"We knew you could do it, Blythe!" Zoe said. "No one has more talent than you!"

"*Or* works harder," Russell added.

From her smile, the pets could tell how happy Russell's and Zoe's compliments made Blythe—even if she blushed a little at the same time.

"Three cheers for Blythe!" continued Russell. "Her fashions are going to take Paris—and the world—by storm!"

As the pets began cheering again, Zoe and Minka exchanged a relieved glance. For the first time in days, Russell seemed like his old self again: supportive, friendly, and, most of all, fun. *Maybe all the pressure was getting to him,* Zoe thought. *And now that most of the work is done, Russell can relax and enjoy getting ready for Project FUN-way... instead of stressing out.*

"Thanks, everybody!" Blythe replied when the cheers finally died down. "There's no way I would've gotten it done without all of you. I mean it! I don't know *how* Minka knew just when I needed a snack...and Zoe brought me water before I even realized I was thirsty..."

Blythe knelt down so that she and Russell were face-to-face. "And how can I ever thank you for everything *you've* done?" she asked him. "Knowing that you were taking care of all the details for the show let me focus on creating all the new outfits. None of it would've been possible without you."

Russell puffed up with pride. "Well, you know," he said, sounding a little embarrassed, "whatever it takes to make Project FUN-way a success! So...when can we see your new creations?"

Blythe pretended to check her watch. "I don't know," she said playfully. "How about...right now!"

"Oh, thank *goodness*!" Zoe gushed. "I was worried that we would have to wait—and to be honest, I don't think I could wait another *moment*!"

"But, Zoe, haven't you seen them already?" asked Vinnie. "You've been in and out of Blythe's sewing room..."

Zoe shrugged. "Oh, sure, maybe I got a glimpse of a scrap of fabric here, a snip of trim there," she said, waving her paw in the air. "But I haven't seen even one entire outfit!"

"Then what are we waiting for?" asked Penny Ling.

"This way, this way," Russell said as he herded the pets over to the side. "Make room for Blythe! Don't crowd her! Move along!"

A funny expression crossed Blythe's face. She'd never heard Russell talk like that—*especially* not to the other pets at Day Camp. "No, it's okay. I'm fine," she said lightly. "Hang on just a minute, and I'll be right back with my new designs."

The pets waited patiently—or *tried* to wait patiently. For some, like Minka, being patient was easier said than done!

At last, Blythe returned, pushing a rolling clothing rack alongside her. Seven perfectly pressed outfits hung neatly in a row.

Blythe took a deep breath. "I present to you Blythe Style's newest collection— Courage Couture!" she announced proudly.

"Ooh, Blythe! It's fabulous!" cried Zoe.

"I love it already!" added Penny Ling.

"You have outdone yourself!" Sunil chimed in.

As everyone rushed over to examine each outfit, Russell realized that this was the perfect opportunity to talk to Blythe alone. "Blythe, now that all the outfits are finished, do you have a minute to talk about my plans for Project FUN-way?" he asked in a low voice.

"Sure," replied Blythe. "Whenever you want."

Russell beckoned for Blythe to follow him to the opposite end of Day Camp. "Everyone's had a lot of…ideas," he began. Then he paused as Blythe yawned suddenly, covering her mouth with her hand.

"Sorry," she apologized. "I haven't exactly been getting enough sleep lately. Go on."

"As I was saying, everyone's had a lot of ideas. Some good, some not so good…and some *terrible*," Russell explained.

Blythe looked surprised. "Terrible?" she

repeated. Had Russell really said something so harsh about their friends' ideas for the fashion show?

"*Terrible*," Russell repeated emphatically—totally misreading Blythe's expression. "You'll see for yourself. I wrote them all down in my notebook. I didn't want to hurt anyone's feelings or anything. But there is *absolutely* no way they should be part of Project FUN-way!"

Blythe frowned. "But, Russell, we're all working together to pull off this show," she said. "Don't you think that *everyone* should be able to contribute?"

Russell made a face. "Not this time, Blythe. Project FUN-way is too important. The stakes are too high. Remember, this is your reputation on the line—in front of the entire world! Trust me! I'm in charge, and I take that very seriously!"

Blythe wasn't sure how to respond. On the one hand, she truly believed that *every-one's* ideas were important. It didn't seem right for Russell to ignore them. But on the other hand, she knew how hard he had been working behind the scenes to organize every last little detail for Project FUN-way.

Before Blythe could respond, Russell pressed his notebook into her hands. "Now, here are all the notes and requirements for the show," he explained. "If there's an *X* next to it, e-mail it to Mona Autumn's people in Paris so that they can take care of the arrangements before we arrive. But if there's a star next to it, just ignore it."

"*X*—e-mail. Star—ignore," Blythe

repeated as she stifled another yawn. "I'll send this e-mail first thing tomorrow morning. For now, I think I'm going to go home and go to bed early for a change."

"No! Blythe, you've got to send it tonight!" he exclaimed. "Remember, it's six hours later in Paris...so if you send it tonight, the team can get right to work tomorrow morning. Otherwise, they might not have a chance to get started until tomorrow night, or the next day, which is really the day *after* tomorrow, or otherwise known as next Tuesday, which might not be enough time, especially since we need to—"

Blythe held up her hands. All of Russell's talk about dates and times was making her tired head swim! "Okay, okay, I'll send it tonight," she said. "Just let me get all the outfits pressed and packed first..."

"I'll handle that," Russell said reassuringly. "You go send the e-mail. And then go right to bed!"

"Thanks," Blythe said gratefully. "I really appreciate your hard work, Russell. I don't know what I'd do without you."

After she said good-bye to the pets and Mrs. Twombly, Blythe snuck out the back entrance of the Littlest Pet Shop. It was the only way to get back to her own apartment without being mobbed by all her brand-new fans!

"Hey, there's my favorite internationally famous fashion designer!" Roger announced with a grin as she walked in the door. He was wearing a bright red apron, and from the smell of garlic and tomatoes in the air, Blythe could tell he was making one of her favorite dinners: spaghetti and meatballs. "Hope you're hungry. I think I made enough for an army!"

"It smells great, Dad," Blythe said dreamily, with another yawn. "How long until dinner?"

Roger stirred the sauce in the pot with a wooden spoon. Then he took a tiny taste. "Mmm, perfect!" he announced. "We'll eat in five minutes. Would you set the table, please?"

Blythe paused. She'd promised Russell that she would send the e-mail immediately...but her dad had worked hard to cook her favorite dinner. *I guess the e-mail can wait a little while,* she finally decided. *Besides, I am pretty hungry.*

As soon as dinner was over, Blythe helped clear the table and do the dishes. Then she went to her bedroom, where she powered up her laptop. While she waited for her e-mail to load, Blythe opened Russell's notebook. He had scribbled notes all over the first page . . . and the second page . . . and the *third* page . . .

Wow, Blythe thought. *Is this* all *for the fashion show?* Blythe scrunched up her face as she flipped through the pages. Sure enough, each page was covered with Russell's plans for Project FUN-way. He'd made notes about *everything*—from the theme to the backdrop to the travel arrangements to the lighting! Blythe could tell that Russell had worked incredibly hard—all to help her.

But as Blythe kept flipping through the notebook, she started to worry. *This almost seems like* too *much,* Blythe thought. *What if the Paris organizers think we're bossing them around? What if they feel like we don't trust them to know how to put on a fashion show? What if they think I'm some kind of diva or something?*

Blythe shook her head. *Russell knows what he's doing,* she reminded herself. *He wouldn't go to all this trouble for nothing. I'll just have to figure out the right way to ask for all these requests. But first, I have to figure out which ones Russell wanted me to send.*

Blythe squinted at the page. It wasn't easy to tell which marks were Xs and which ones were stars. All the smudgy, scraggly marks Russell had made looked pretty similar— even in the light of Blythe's brightest lamp.

Those are probably the stars, Blythe finally decided. She started typing an e-mail to one of Mona Autumn's assistants.

***Bonjour*, Marie!**

I am so excited to send these
requests for the fashion show. I
know this list is long, so if any of our
requests are too difficult, feel free
to switch them out for something
easier. The new outfits are finished,
too—so we're just about ready to
leave! Thank you for everything,
Marie—or should I say, *merci
beaucoup*?

XOXO,
Blythe

Then Blythe typed up the long list of
notes Russell had made, from sparkly tinsel

curtains to spotlights in every color to tra-
pcze artists to *fireballs*! There was no doubt
in her mind that Project FUN-way was
going to be exciting—and "exciting" was an
understatement!

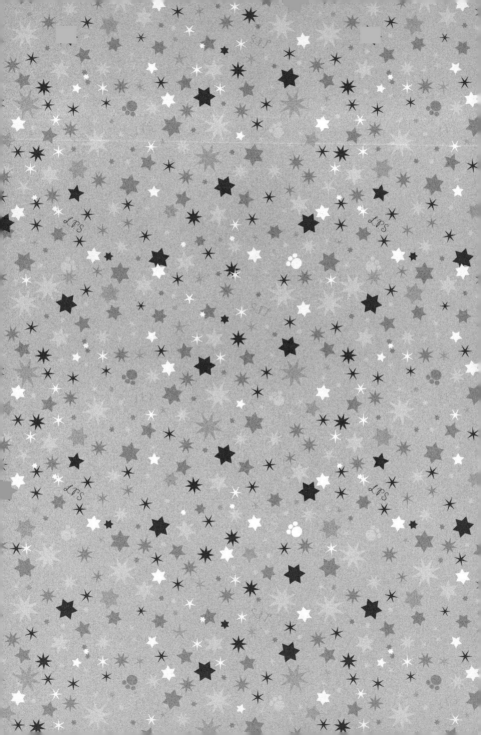

Chapter 6

Just twenty-four hours later, Blythe and the pets boarded the Pet Jet and settled in for an overnight flight to Paris. The past several days had been a whirlwind of hard work and long hours. Now it was time to relax... and have fun!

Blythe glanced out one of the paw-print-shaped windows, where she could see the beautiful sunset cast golden light over all the buildings in Downtown City. *It's so crazy,* she thought with a smile. *The next time we see the sun, it will be morning in Paris!*

"Attention, this is your captain speaking." Roger's voice crackled over the speakers. "Please prepare for takeoff."

The plane's door closed and locked with a loud *whoosh.* Blythe glanced around the jet. "Is everybody's seat belt buckled?" she asked as she did a quick head count. "Wait a second—I only see six seats filled. Who's missing?"

"I'm here," Zoe called.

"Me too," added Sunil.

"And me three!" Vinnie piped up.

"There's Pepper, Penny Ling, and Minka," Blythe said as she counted the others. "Which means...Russell's not here!"

As the engine rumbled, Blythe scrambled out of her seat and sprinted over to the intercom. "Dad! Dad!" she said urgently. "Don't leave yet. We're not quite ready."

"What's the problem?" Roger replied over the speaker. "We've already been cleared for takeoff."

"Russell's not here," Blythe explained. "We can't leave without him. Let me—"

Suddenly, Zoe hopped onto the armrest of her seat. "I see him!" she shrieked. "Russell's still on the runway!"

"What!" Blythe cried. "What's he doing out there?"

She rushed over and looked out the window beside Zoe. Sure enough, the hedgehog was perched on a baggage cart, watching carefully as the baggage handlers finished loading the last of the luggage onto the Pet Jet.

Blythe went back to the intercom. "It's okay, Dad—we found him," she reported. "But Russell's still out on the tarmac! Can you open the door again?"

"Out on the tarmac!" Roger exclaimed. "Do you mean to tell me we almost flew to Paris—and left Russell behind?"

"I don't know how it happened," Blythe said. "But I'll personally make sure that *everyone* is on board with their seat belts fastened before we take off."

"I'll open the door now," Roger said, "but be careful on the tarmac, Blythe. It's no place to fool around."

"I totally agree," Blythe said, her mouth set in a frown as she stared at Russell through the window.

As soon as the door opened, Blythe hurried down the steps.

"Whoops, coming through, pardon me," she said as she darted and dodged past the baggage handlers. She swooped down and gathered Russell into her arms. "Russell!" she hissed. "What were you thinking?"

"Oh, hi, Blythe," Russell replied. "What's the matter?"

"What's the matter?" she repeated in disbelief. "We could've left without you—that's what's the matter! Why are you still on the tarmac when everyone else is ready for takeoff?"

"Well, *somebody* had to make sure that all the luggage was properly loaded onto the Pet Jet," Russell explained calmly. "Can you *imagine* if one of the bags had been left behind? Or one of your new outfits? The horror!"

"The real horror would've been leaving

you behind," Blythe retorted. "Besides, the baggage handlers know what they're doing. You can trust them to get the job done."

Just then, Blythe noticed that one of the baggage handlers was giving her a strange look. She turned to the side so that he couldn't see her talking to Russell, who was shaking his head.

"No way, Blythe—not this time," Russell said. "I'm in charge, and I—"

"—take that very seriously," Blythe finished for him with a sigh.

As soon as they were on board the Pet Jet, Russell climbed into his seat and fastened his seat belt. When Blythe was certain that *all* the pets were on board at last, she told her father that they were ready for takeoff. The engine roared to life as the plane taxied down the runway. Then, all of a sudden, it lifted into the sky! A giant grin crossed Blythe's face as she stared out the window. No matter how many times Blythe flew somewhere on the Pet Jet, she always loved the swoopy thrill she felt when the plane took off. As the plane flew higher into the sky, the giant buildings of Downtown City started to look like miniature toys. Soon the plane would soar over the ocean, with only the twinkling stars and gleaming moon to light the way.

Zoe pushed a button to make her seat recline. "Time for a little beauty rest," she announced. "But don't worry, I made sure my owners packed my Blythe Style sleep mask and my Blythe Style earmuffs in my carry-on bag. So feel free to make as much noise as you want—you won't bother me."

"Hey, look!" Vinnie yelled excitedly.

"They're showing *Space Lizards: Race Against Time* tonight. I've been wanting to see that movie for ages!"

"Me too!" Sunil said.

"Anybody want some snacks?" Minka spoke up.

"Well, yeah—of course!" Vinnie said. "Aren't snacks the whole point of watching a movie?"

"Great! I'll get some as soon as Blythe's dad turns off the fasten-seat-belt sign!" Minka said excitedly.

"Ahem." Russell cleared his throat to get everyone's attention. But the other pets were chattering so much that no one noticed.

"Blythe, would you paint my nails?" Penny Ling asked. "I think my owner meant to do it, but she ran out of time."

"Sure," replied Blythe. One of the best things about a night flight on the Pet Jet was that it felt more like a sleepover party than an airplane ride! "What color do you want?"

"Ahem!" Russell said again, louder this time.

"Ooh, mine too!" Pepper spoke up. "I have this really pretty glitter nail polish. It kind of looks like fireworks! So it will be perfect for—"

"*Ahem!*" Russell shouted at the top of his lungs. Everyone turned to stare at him. "These are all very good plans...for the flight home. But for now, we've got work to do!"

Everyone stared at him blankly.

"What do you mean?" Blythe asked in confusion. "Everything's packed and loaded…Marie e-mailed me back this morning to say that the Paris team is handling all the setup on the ground…we're literally forty thousand feet in the air. How can we have work to do?"

"We never *practiced*," Russell explained. "You know, all those important fashion show moves. How to work it on the runway, how to strike a pose, how to swivel and turn at just the right moment…"

"Oh. I guess you're right," Blythe replied. "But I'm sure we'll have time tomorrow for a quick run-through before the show starts."

"But what if we *don't*?" Russell argued. "This is way too important to leave up to chance like that, Blythe! To be honest, I'm surprised by your attitude. I'd think that *you* of all people would care about the show as much as *I* do!"

"Of *course* I care about the show," Blythe said, stung. "But I also care about everybody getting the chance to take a break... relax... even rest a little."

"Yeah, Russell," Vinnie spoke up. "You really should think about taking Blythe's advice. Especially the relaxing part."

"We can relax when the show is over," Russell said firmly. He wasn't going to back down—not an inch. "But as soon as Blythe's dad turns off the fasten-seat-belt sign—"

Ding!

Everyone looked up as the seat-belt sign suddenly went dark. Roger's voice crackled over the speaker once more. "Good evening," he said. "We've reached our cruising altitude of forty-two thousand feet, with clear skies ahead. Feel free to move about the cabin, and enjoy your flight!"

Russell clapped his paws together. "Everybody up!" he announced.

Blythe tried not to sigh. *Enjoy our flight? Not likely,* she thought as, one by one, the pets unbuckled their seat belts and joined Russell in the aisle—all except Zoe. With her Blythe Style sleep mask and earmuffs, she'd missed the entire conversation!

"You too, Zoe," Russell called. But Zoe still snoozed, entirely oblivious until Russell marched right over to her and snapped the sleep mask off her head!

"Huh—what—*hey!*" Zoe yelped. "What's going on?"

"Sorry to wake you, Zoe, but we've got a lot of practicing to do," Russell told her.

"Practicing?" Zoe asked in a grumpy-sounding voice. "You woke me up to *practice?*

Darling, have you forgotten that I've done this before? I've modeled in pet shows all over the world! I'll be fine tomorrow—don't you worry."

Before Zoe could flop back in her seat and drift off to dreamland again, Russell stopped her. "Oh, I'm sure that you can handle it, Zoe," he said in a quiet voice. "But...can they?"

He pointed over to the aisle, where Vinnie and Sunil had already started practicing their best modeling moves—with hilariously awful results! Every time Vinnie struck a pose, he snapped his tongue at someone. It was obvious that Vinnie thought he looked extra cool...but the slimy drool on his tongue pretty much ruined the effect. Meanwhile, Sunil spent so much time trying to dodge Vinnie's crazy flying tongue that he started weaving back and forth in the aisle, knocking into Penny Ling, who then stumbled into Pepper, who accidentally stomped on Minka's tail!

"Hmm," Zoe replied as the other pets tried to untangle themselves. "I see what you mean."

"With a little coaching from us, I know we can get everyone runway-ready by the time this plane lands in Paris," Russell declared.

Blythe shook her head. "I don't know, Russell," she said. "A good night's sleep might be just as useful as a whole night of practice. Don't you think that everybody deserves a little break before the big show?"

"There will be *plenty* of time to relax and have fun at the after-party, Blythe,"

Russell said firmly. Then he clapped his paws together. "Okay! I want everyone to make a single-file line by the cockpit. When I call your name, I want you to walk down the aisle just like you would during the show. Zoe and I will give you notes about how you can improve your modeling moves. Vinnie! You're up!"

Blythe settled into one of the seats to watch the rehearsal, but she didn't look happy about it.

And neither did the pets.

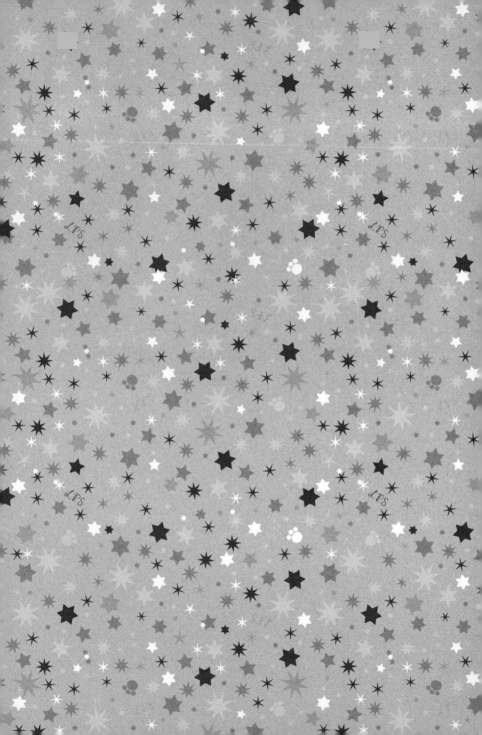

Chapter 7

Eight hours later, the Pet Jet landed at the Paris airport. After a long night of practicing, Russell was finally pleased with the pets' modeling moves. But he was the only one with a smile on his face. Everyone else was tired, grumpy, worn out—and ready for a long nap at the hotel.

"Look over there," Blythe said, pointing through the window as the plane taxied down the runway. "It's our hotel. So we'll be able to check in and get a little rest just as soon as we get off the plane."

"Not so fast, Blythe," Russell said. "We have to make sure everything's ready for the show first."

This time, though, Blythe was ready to put her foot down. "Russell. No. Everyone needs to rest," she argued. "Or else they'll be too tired to model on the runway—let alone have any fun tonight! Remember, this is Project *FUN*-way."

"Blythe, check it out," Zoe spoke up suddenly. "It looks like there are some people here to see you."

Blythe turned in her seat to glance through Zoe's window. Sure enough, a group of *Tres Blasé* staffers were waiting on the tarmac beside a large purple tent.

"Wow—that's Mona Autumn, right in front! I can't believe she came here to meet our plane! And check out that tent over there—I bet that's where they're holding Project FUN-way!" Blythe exclaimed.

The grouchiness in the cabin was immediately replaced by cheers. The fashion show and awards ceremony suddenly seemed more real than ever. Everyone was filled with anticipation and excitement—everyone except Russell.

"A purple tent?" he asked, sounding confused. "The tent's not supposed to be purple. I specifically said a silver tent. *Silver.*"

"What does it matter?" asked Vinnie. "Silver, purple, or plaid with polka dots—a tent is a tent."

Russell took a deep breath, trying not to lose his temper. "It matters because I have a *vision* for the show," he said slowly. "And if the tent's wrong, maybe the lights are wrong. If the lights are wrong, maybe the backdrop's wrong. And if the backdrop's wrong—"

"Russell, don't look for problems when there aren't any," Blythe told him, trying to sound reassuring. "*Tres Blasé* is a huge international magazine. They host fashion shows all the time. I'm sure they know what they're doing."

Russell crossed his arms over his chest. "Well, I can tell you one thing," he said firmly. "I am *not* going to the hotel until I personally check all the preparations for the show myself. Honestly! Sometimes I think that I'm the only one who even *cares* about Project FUN-way!"

Zoe bristled. She couldn't take any more of Russell's attitude. "Listen up!" she said hotly. But before she could continue, Blythe placed a calming hand on Zoe's back.

"I know this has been really hard," Blythe whispered close to Zoe's ear. "But I'm sure Russell will be back to his usual self as soon as the show gets under way. Let's try to be patient with him—just for a little while longer. I think all the pressure has really gotten to him."

"But, Blythe, it's just not fair!" Zoe whispered back. "How *dare* he imply that he's the only one who cares about the show?"

"I know that, and you know that—and deep down, I bet even Russell knows that," Blythe said. "Let's all just focus on getting through the next few hours. Face it, we're all exhausted. Nobody's at their best right now. We'll get some rest, and before you know it, you'll all be getting dressed up in the new outfits, and the lights will be shining on you, and you'll be walking down the catwalk at Project FUN-way, and all of this will feel so silly and trivial compared to how exciting and amazing that will be!"

A small smile flickered across Zoe's face. "It will be amazing, won't it?" she said. "Everyone's going to go crazy for your new designs, Blythe! I can't wait!"

"Neither can I," Blythe replied as the plane finally came to a stop. She straightened her skirt and adjusted Zoe's beret as the door whooshed open. "Come on! Let's go greet our friends from *Tres Blasé*!"

Blythe and her dad were the first ones to exit the plane, with the pets filing behind them in a row.

"Blythe! Darling! So good to see you again," Mona Autumn said as she kissed the air near Blythe's face. "And are these all your little models? How adorable!"

One of Mona Autumn's assistants looked worried. "Um...shouldn't they be in carriers?" he asked anxiously.

Mona shot him a look. "Do you mean cages? Like they're...animals?" she asked in a withering voice. "I would never treat our models like that. *Never.*"

"It's all right. I can assure you that they're all very well trained," Blythe said. "Allow me to introduce Zoe, Pepper, Penny Ling, Minka, Vinnie, and Sunil. And I'm sure you remember...Russell? Russell? Has anyone seen Russell?"

"Maybc hc's still on the plane," suggested Sunil.

But Blythe shook her head. "He's not on the plane," she said. "He's in the tent."

All eyes turned toward the purple tent, where they could see Russell's prickly silhouette. No one spoke as he turned around and scurried over to the group as fast as his little legs could carry him.

"WRONG!" he howled at the top of his lungs. "Wrong, wrong, wrong, *wrong*! *It's—all—WRONG!*"

To Blythe and the pets, every angry word coming out of Russell's mouth was crystal clear. But to everyone else on the tarmac, all they saw was a furious little hedgehog, chattering and squeaking frantically as he jumped up and down. Some of Mona Autumn's assistants started to giggle.

"Are you sure we don't need a carrier?" someone asked. "Or at least a leash?"

"He is rather wild, isn't he?" Mona asked. "I don't remember quite that much...personality from him before."

"Isn't he a cutie?" cooed another assistant. "I just want to give him a squishy hug and make him feel all better!"

Someone else wrinkled her nose. "Too grouchy. I like happy pets better."

"This is dreadful!" Zoe growled under her breath. "Russell is making a fool of us in front of the entire staff of *Tres Blasé*! We've got to stop him!"

"I know exactly what this situation needs," Vinnie announced. "A distraction!"

"I said *satin* curtains! *Satin!*" Russell howled.

Just then, Vinnie leaped off the ground and sailed over Russell's head. In midair, he struck his best pose from the all-night practice session. Some of the staffers gasped…but they started giggling again when Vinnie crashed into the baggage cart.

"That was…unexpected," Mona Autumn said.

"I, um, I can explain," Blythe said helplessly. But before she could say another word, Russell continued his tantrum.

"And those lights—*unacceptable*! I was *very clear* about the lights! All white spotlights! None of this rainbow-light *nonsense*!" he yelled.

"Russell…" Blythe began.

Penny Ling grabbed a red velvet rope that marked off a special area for the press to take photos. "This might work for a quick ribbon dance," she said. "At the least, it should take everyone's attention off Russell."

"Ooh, great idea! I'll be your music!"
Minka announced. As Penny Ling flung out
her arm to make the rope soar through the
air, Minka started singing. But to the people
gathered around, Minka's singing sounded
more like hooting and howling. Meanwhile,
the red velvet rope was too heavy for a beautiful, delicate ribbon dance. It thunked on
the tarmac like a long link of sausages.

One of the *Tres Blasé* staffers grimaced.
"That was *painful*," he muttered under his
breath. And worst of all, the distractions
weren't working. Russell's tantrum got bigger and louder with every passing second.
No one could look away—not even Mona
Autumn herself.

"Blythe," Mona said, "is he quite all
right? Should I call a vet?"

"He's fine," Blythe said shortly. Then

she buried her head in her hands. Zoe was right—this was more than a debacle. It was a disaster. There was only one thing for Blythe to do—and in that moment, she realized that she should've done it days ago.

"Russell," Blythe said firmly. She knelt down so that she and Russell could see eye-to-eye. "Russell. *RUSSELL!*"

At last, Blythe had Russell's attention. It was too bad that she'd had to yell to get it.

"This has gone too far," Blythe said. "*Way* too far. You can't treat people like this, Russell. You can't treat your friends like this. It's not right."

"Blythe! I thought *you* of all people would understand!" he howled in response. "They've gone and done the exact *opposite* of everything I planned for the show. All those terrible ideas from everybody else—"

"What do you mean, *terrible ideas?*" Zoe asked. But Blythe held up a finger to quiet her.

Russell's eyes grew wide. "Wait a minute," he said slowly. "Wait—just—one—minute. How did the people at *Tres Blasé* even know about everybody else's ideas?"

Blythe thought back to the night when she'd e-mailed Marie. She remembered how tired she'd been...and how she wasn't *quite* sure she knew which marks were stars and which marks were Xs...and her face went pale.

"I, uh...well...I may have sent the wrong list," she admitted. "I'm sorry."

Russell took a deep breath—the perfect fuel for an even louder and longer tantrum. But before he could get started, Blythe took both of his paws in her hands.

"It was an accident," she continued. "And you know what? Project FUN-way is still going to be amazing—even if the lighting's not exactly the way you dreamed it would be, or if the tent is the wrong color. Because we all worked incredibly hard to make this happen. We're all together in Paris—the fashion capital of the world! It's amazing, isn't it?"

Russell stared at the ground for a long moment. "Yeah. I guess," he said. "But, Blythe, can't you talk to Mona Autumn? Can't you tell her there was a terrible mistake, and we really, really need to get my silver sawhorses instead, and also a—"

Blythe shook her head. "No, Russell," she said gently. "Everyone at *Tres Blasé* has worked just as hard as we did. And if you're not careful, you're going to end up hurting a lot of feelings. Come on. Let's go check in to the hotel. I have a sneaking suspicion that everything will look better after a big breakfast and a little rest."

"Maybe," Russell replied—but he didn't sound convinced. All his spines prickled with unhappiness as he watched everyone line up for the tram. Russell knew that he would have to join them. He didn't have a choice.

Or did he?

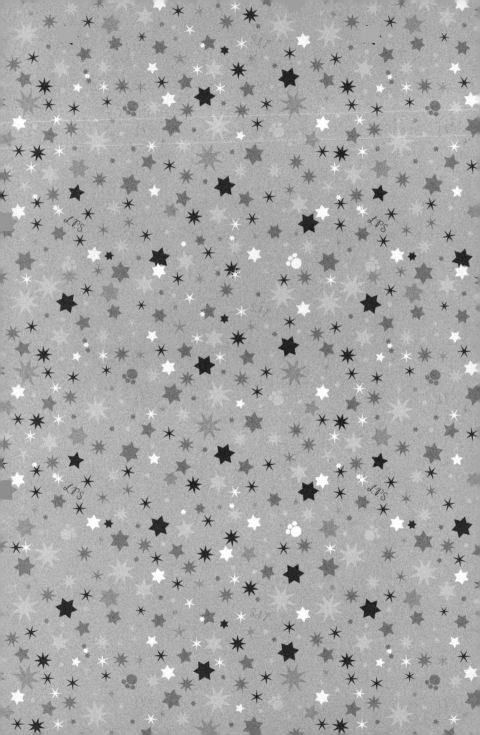

Chapter 8

There was so much commotion as Blythe, Roger, Mona Autumn, the *Tres Blasé* staffers, and the pets prepared to board the tram that no one noticed as Russell took one last, wistful glance at the purple tent.

How can Project FUN-way go on without the right kind of tent? Or the perfect lights? he thought sadly. He'd imagined it so clearly. Everything was going to be just right.

And now? It felt more like everything was going to be ruined. Worst of all, no one seemed to care. They were all chatting and laughing as they climbed aboard the tram, as if they didn't even mind that Russell's vision for the show had been ruined.

Maybe it's not too late, Russell thought suddenly. *I'm not tired. If I skipped the hotel and went into the city instead... maybe I could find just what we need to make the show perfect after all.*

Russell glanced around. Normally, he would take a while to really think through his options and figure out the very best thing to do. But there wasn't a lot of time for him to decide. The tram would be heading off to the hotel at any moment...

In an instant, Russell made up his mind. He scurried in the opposite direction and leaped onto the baggage cart. Russell nestled himself between two suitcases so no one could see him. From his hiding place, Russell took a quick peek at the tarmac. The last few people were about to board the tram to the hotel. Russell waited, hardly daring to breathe, for someone to notice he was missing.

But in all the commotion, no one did.

When the luggage cart lurched forward, Russell breathed a sigh of relief. He was on his way to save the show! This was no time for relaxing, though. As the cart approached the airport, Russell knew that he had to stay alert. The last thing he needed was someone noticing a lone hedgehog roaming the streets of Paris, all by himself. Luckily, Russell was small enough that it was easy for him to stay out of sight. There was so much hustle and bustle at the airport, with travelers rushing to catch their flights, that no one paid much attention to Russell at all—not even when he hitched a ride on a rolling suitcase and snuck into the back of a taxi that took him straight to the heart of Paris!

Standing on the cobblestone street, surrounded by fashionable boutiques and elegant cafés, Russell took a deep breath. He could smell fresh bread, beautiful flowers, and the aromas of coffee and chocolate. The entire city seemed magical—like a place where anything could happen. For the first time in days, Russell forgot all about Project FUN-way—for a moment, at least. *I want to see everything!* he thought excitedly. *I wish everybody else was here, too. I wish we could all explore Paris together.*

Russell shook his head. *Focus, Russell!* he scolded himself. *It's up to* you *to save Project FUN-way and make it as amazing as you know it can be! That's the most important thing. In fact, it's the* only *thing!*

Russell tried to figure out what he needed first. That's when he realized something: His important notebook, filled with every idea he'd had for Project FUN-way, was still in Blythe's carry-on bag!

"*Arrgghh!*" Russell groaned in frustration. Without his notebook, he'd have to try to remember every single thing he wanted to have at the show. But that was *hundreds* of items! Russell started to rack his brain, trying to remember the most important props for the show. *Those exposed clear lightbulbs,* he thought suddenly. *Lighting is a* really *big deal at a fashion show. And the silver sawhorses... I could probably find some regular ones and paint them silver... but then I'd also need silver paint... and would the paint even dry in time for the show? Minka would know! I wish she was here!*

Russell sighed. *One thing at a time,* he told himself. *Lightbulbs first!*

Everyone knew that Paris was the fashion capital of the world. Russell figured that must make it the shopping capital of the world, too. There was just one problem: Paris was also an enormous city... and Russell didn't know how to find anything. The stores on this particular street sold gorgeous dresses, fancy shoes, and expensive perfumes. *Wow, Blythe and Zoe have* got *to see this!* Russell thought excitedly as he peeked into one store filled with glamorous gowns. But his smile faded when he realized that his friends were all the way back at the hotel. There was no denying it: It would've been a lot more fun to explore Paris with his pals.

Russell checked store after store, but none of them sold lightbulbs, let alone sawhorses or silver paint.

No big deal, Russell thought as he tried to reassure himself. *I bet they'll be selling something I need on the next street... or the one just beyond that...* but even though Russell roamed the streets of Paris for hours, he never found what he was looking for... or anything close to it. *Don't get discouraged,* he thought, trying to give himself a pep talk to keep his spirits up. It would've been easier if Pepper had been there to make him laugh. *Or Penny Ling,* Russell thought sadly. *Somehow, Penny Ling always knows just what to say when I'm feeling bad about something.*

After Russell hitched a ride on a bus, he arrived in a completely different section of the city. Gone were the little boutiques, sidewalk cafés, and cobblestone streets. Now Russell was surrounded by sleek, glittering skyscrapers that reached high into the sky. *Where am I?* he wondered. The truth was that Russell had no idea.

Surrounded by people hurrying past him on the sidewalk, Russell suddenly felt all alone in the world.

Chapter 9

A few hours later, Blythe awoke in an enormous bed with sheer canopy curtains. As she stretched and yawned, it took her half a second to remember where she was: a hotel in Paris, on the day of the Project FUN-way fashion show!

In an instant, Blythe was out of bed and

on her feet, all traces of sleepiness forgotten in the excitement of the moment. "Guys! Guys! *Guys!*" she cried excitedly. "Wake up! Project FUN-way starts in *two hours!*"

From cozy pet beds scattered around the elegant hotel room, all the pets awoke. Just like Blythe, their jet lag immediately transformed into excitement.

Blythe's phone started buzzing. "I just got a text from Mona," she announced. "Guess what? It's just about time to start getting ready!"

Zoe clapped her paws together. "Oh, I can't *wait!*" she said delightedly. "Getting ready for a fashion show is my favorite part!"

"Really?" Minka teased her. "I thought your favorite part was getting your picture taken."

"I thought your favorite part was walking the runway," added Sunil.

"And *I* thought your favorite part was the after-party," joked Vinnie.

"What can I say?" Zoe asked with a laugh. "They're *all* my favorite parts!"

"I can't believe it's here at last!" Blythe exclaimed. "It's all felt like a dream—and now it's coming true!"

"So…" Penny Ling began, sounding a little uncertain. "Should we change into our outfits here?"

"Yeah," added Pepper. "What happens next? Some of us haven't done this modeling thing as often as others."

Zoe immediately took charge. "Not to worry, darlings. You're working with a seasoned professional," she assured them.

"We'll go right over to that great big tent on the tarmac. There will be a special VIP-only section, just for us. That stands for *Very Important Pets*, you know."

Vinnie's eyes lit up. "Very Important Pets? I could get used to that!" he said.

"It's going to be *fabulous*," Zoe assured him. "The best grooming you've ever had in your entire life! Hair, makeup—oh, and lots of *delicious* snacks—"

"This is sounding better and better!" Sunil chimed in.

"And *then*, once everybody's ready, we'll change into Blythe's wonderful outfits and get ready to show the world just what Blythe can do!" Zoe continued.

"Thanks, Zoe," Blythe said. "And on that note, we'll do one last wardrobe check before we head down to the tent!"

Blythe crossed the room to a rolling rack, where she had carefully hung each outfit before collapsing into bed. "Let's see," she began. "Zoe...Penny Ling...Sunil... Vinnie...Minka...Pepper...Russell..."

One by one, each pet stepped forward to take the outfit from Blythe—except for Russell.

Blythe glanced around the room. "Russell?" she repeated. A frown crossed her face. "Has anyone seen Russell?"

The pets looked around, too.

"Actually, now that you mention it...no," Zoe said, shaking her head.

"Well, he's gotta be here somewhere!" Pepper announced as she poked her head under the bed. "Russell! Where are you?"

"He's not on the balcony," Sunil reported.

"He's not in the bathroom, either," added Vinnie.

A deep feeling of worry settled over Blythe. "Has *anyone* seen him since we were on the tarmac?" she asked urgently. "The last time I remember seeing him was outside the tent—"

"When he pitched that great, big, giant fit," Minka remembered.

Silence fell over the room as all the pets tried to remember the last time they'd seen Russell. In the long pause that followed, it was obvious that no one had seen Russell since his tantrum. At some point since then, he had disappeared...and now no one knew where he was.

Blythe swallowed hard. "How could this happen?" she asked. "I thought we *all* checked in to the hotel together. But—how—oh, I feel just terrible!"

Zoe rushed over to her. "Now, now, Blythe, you can't blame yourself," she said soothingly. "It's been absolutely crazy busy and exhausting, and we've *all* been more scattered than usual."

"Yeah," Vinnie chimed in. "What we have to do now is figure out where Russell went."

"Does anybody have any ideas?" asked Sunil.

"Well...he was really upset about the arrangements for the show," Blythe said thoughtfully. "There was that big mix-up, and...I think...I think Russell was determined to make his vision for Project FUNway happen...even though the Paris team didn't get the props and lighting he requested. I tried to tell him that the show would still be phenomenal, but..."

"He was awfully determined, wasn't

he?" asked Penny Ling. "You know Russell. When he gets his mind set on something, he doesn't let anything stand in his way."

"Are you suggesting that Russell decided to find a way to get the props he wanted?" asked Blythe. "But—that would mean—"

"Going shopping in Paris—all by himself!" cried Zoe. "*Nobody* should shop Paris alone! *Nobody!*"

"It's not the shopping I'm worried about," Blythe said. "It's Russell, all by himself in a strange city...a *big* city..." Blythe stood up abruptly. "Well, as they say, the show must go on," she began. "But *not* without Russell. Come on, guys! We've got to figure out a way to find Russell and bring him back!"

"How would we get into the city?" asked Minka. "Call a taxi? Take the subway?"

"I have another idea," Blythe said as she grabbed her phone. "Hello? Dad? We have an emergency! Russell is missing...I think he's in the city...yes...yes! That's exactly what I was thinking! Thanks, Dad!"

When Blythe turned back to the pets, her eyes were shining with hope. "Dad's going to get special permission to fly us over Paris in one of the airport's helicopters," she said breathlessly. "With a bird's-eye view, I'm sure we can spot Russell!"

"Hooray!" all the pets cheered as they jumped up and down.

"Come on, everybody," Blythe said. "Let's change into our outfits here, tell Mona Autumn everything, and then hit the skies with Dad to find Russell! Let's do it!"

Moments later, Blythe dashed out of the hotel room in a search-and-rescue uniform, with all the pets scurrying behind her. They found Mona Autumn in the middle of the tent, barking orders into her headset. She started applauding when she saw Blythe and the pets in their outfits.

"Blythe, *darling*, you've outdone yourself!" Mona began.

"We have a problem," Blythe said in a rush. "One of my models is missing, and the show can't start without him."

Mona waved her hand in the air. "That's not a problem," she said in an airy voice. "Models can easily be replaced."

"Not this one," Blythe said firmly. "Not Russell the hedgehog. Because he isn't just one of my models ... he's one of my friends."

For the first time, Blythe truly had Mona's attention. "The hedgehog?" she exclaimed in alarm. "But he's a fan favorite!

Enormously popular! The whole wide world will be watching for him tonight! Don't tell me he got cold paws!"

Blythe shook her head. "No…I think there's something else going on," she replied.

Mona started pacing. "Just like there would be no show without Blythe, I don't see how we can have a show without Russell," she announced. "You two are the dream team that sold all those copies of *Tres Blasé*. If—"

"We have a plan to find him," Blythe spoke up, interrupting Mona Autumn for the first time ever. "My dad's going to fly us over Paris in a helicopter."

Blythe held her breath as she waited for Mona's response. If Mona canceled the show now, after everything they'd been through…

"All right," Mona finally agreed. "But you're taking one of my photographers with you. If the show *can't* go on, at least we'll have some high-action shots of your adventures for the next issue of *Tres Blasé*."

"Fine! Absolutely! No problem!" Blythe exclaimed. Then she turned to the pets. "Come on, everybody! Let's go!"

Across the tarmac, Roger was testing the controls of the helicopter. Blythe helped all the pets board the chopper before she climbed on, too.

"Ready to go?" Roger asked as he fiddled with his headset.

Blythe shook her head. "Not just yet, Dad," she replied. "Mona wants us to bring a photographer to document our search."

From the way Roger raised an eyebrow, Blythe could tell he thought that was as ridiculous as she did. Just then, a man carrying an expensive camera approached the helicopter. "My name is Marc," he said, with just a hint of a French accent. "Is this the model search-and-rescue mission?"

"It's a search-and-rescue mission for our *friend*," Blythe corrected him. "Hurry. We're about to take off."

The moment Roger was cleared for takeoff, he piloted the helicopter into the sky. "We'll be flying over the heart of Paris in a few minutes," Roger announced to everyone.

Blythe craned her neck as she glanced out the window at the glittering city. From up in the sky, Paris seemed bigger than ever.

How in the world would they find one little hedgehog among all the world-famous landmarks, buildings, people, and pets?

Chapter 10

Meanwhile, in the heart of Paris, the loneliness inside Russell got worse with every passing moment. He didn't know what to do or where to go—but he was certain about one thing: Figuring things out would've been a lot easier with his pals by his side.

I need them, he realized suddenly. *I need them a whole lot more than I need special lightbulbs or silver paint . . . or anything else in the world.*

Just like that, Russell realized how wrong he'd been about Project FUN-way. Somehow, in his eagerness to make everything perfect, he'd forgotten about the fun part . . . and he'd forgotten about his friends' feelings, too.

Blythe was right, he thought. *None of that other stuff matters! And if I don't get back to the airport soon, I'm going to miss the show!*

With his mind made up and his heart full of determination, Russell charged forward.

Then he stopped.

Where is *the airport?* he wondered.

Surrounded by towering skyscrapers that blocked his view in every direction, Russell couldn't tell.

Now Russell was worried—*really* worried.

If I can't find the airport, I can't get back to my friends, he thought anxiously as he started pacing back and forth, back and forth, back and forth on the sidewalk until—

"*Pardonnez-moi!*" a voice said as Russell suddenly collided with someone right on the sidewalk!

"Ow!" Russell yelped as he rubbed his head. "Sorry! So sorry!"

"Russell?" the voice asked in amazement. "Is that *you*?"

Russell looked up—and got the surprise of his life. Somehow, he'd run right into Captain Cuddles! As the elegant European polecat reached out a paw to help Russell up, the hedgehog scrambled to his feet. Despite his shock, Russell was filled with relief to see a familiar face. Captain Cuddles had visited Day Camp a few times in the past, and he and Pepper had discovered that they had special feelings for each other.

"*Oui*, it is I," Captain Cuddles said with a grin. "What brings you to Paris?"

The words tumbled out of Russell in a rush as he explained everything—from the *Tres Blasé* megasales to the Project FUN-way show featuring Blythe's designs to his huge, giant, enormous mistake in putting the show before his pals.

"My, my, my," Captain Cuddles finally said. "You *have* been busy!"

"I've got to make it right," Russell told him. "I've got to tell my friends how sorry I am about the way I've behaved. But I don't even know how to get back to the airport!"

Captain Cuddles's brow furrowed as he thought about it. "Yes, I always find myself hopelessly lost in this part of Paris," he confessed. "But you know what you could do? You could go to the top of the Eiffel Tower! From there, you would have a wonderful view of the entire city and countryside. I am sure you would even be able to see the planes coming and going from the airport!"

As Captain Cuddles pointed, Russell turned around to look. There it was: the Eiffel Tower, in all its graceful beauty, stretching into the sky. It was awfully high . . . and Russell was awfully afraid of heights . . .

Russell swallowed hard. "That's a great idea," he told Captain Cuddles, mustering all the courage he could.

Captain Cuddles glanced around. "My owner has an appointment at the spa," he said in a low voice. "I do not think she would notice if I escorted you there."

"Thank you!" Russell exclaimed gratefully.

As Captain Cuddles led Russell through the bustling streets of Paris, the sun began to set, bathing the entire city in beautiful light. Somehow, it became even more enchanting—but Russell barely noticed. All he could think about was finding his way back to his friends.

"Here we are!" Captain Cuddles announced when they reached the Eiffel Tower. "I wish I could go up with you, but I must return before my owner notices that I have slipped away. It was so good to see you, my friend. Please say hello to everyone for me … especially Pepper."

"I will," Russell promised. "And thanks again—for everything!"

As Captain Cuddles hurried away, Russell stepped inside the Eiffel Tower. Then he snuck onto the elevator and traveled all the way to the top floor. When the elevator doors whooshed open, Russell crept toward the edge of the observation deck. Every last one of his quills was quivering with fear. But despite his nervousness, the view was breathtaking. As Russell gazed at Paris in the twilight, he wished more than ever that his friends were with him. Not only would they appreciate the view, Russell knew that with them by his side he'd feel a lot less anxious about being up so high.

Find the airport, he reminded himself. *Because that's the key to finding my friends.*

As Russell scanned the sky, searching for planes, he missed Paris's transformation into the City of Lights; one by one, the streetlights turned on, followed by lights in all the buildings. But there were some lights that Russell simply couldn't miss: the ones illuminating the Eiffel Tower. The brightness of the spotlights nearly blinded Russell, making him hold on to the railing for dear life as they bathed the Eiffel Tower in brilliant white light.

I can't see! Russell thought in terror as he shook his head and blinked, trying to get his vision back. A wave of dizziness washed over him. *I can't see* anything! *What am I going to do?*

Russell might not have been able to see—but he could still hear. Was that the *chop-chop-chop* of a helicopter?

And was it getting closer?

Russell turned his head toward the sky as the sound got louder and louder. Then, to his amazement, he thought he heard his name.

"Russell!"

That voice was so familiar...

"Russell!"

"Blythe?" Russell yelled to the sky.

"Hang on, Russell!" Blythe cried. "We're coming!"

Hanging on—as tight as he could!—was just about all that Russell could manage. But inside, his heart was full of joy. *They came for me*, Russell thought happily. *My friends are here!*

Slowly, as his vision began to return, Russell could make out the shape of the helicopter as it descended. Soon, it was hovering not far above his head. But how would he get inside?

To Russell's astonishment, a ladder unfurled from the helicopter's entrance. And there was Blythe, looking pale but determined as she began to climb down it in her search-and-rescue outfit!

When their eyes met, Blythe gave Russell an encouraging smile. "This is as close as we can get!" she shouted over the noise of the helicopter. "Do you think you can jump into my arms?"

"I—I—" Russell stammered.

"I *know* you can do it!" Blythe told him. "You can do anything! On the count of three. One...two...*three!*"

Russell took a deep breath, scrunched his eyes closed—

And jumped!

The night air rushed past his face, ruffling his quills as Russell flew through the air. Then, just when he thought he wasn't going to make it, Russell felt Blythe's arms wrap tightly around him.

"I got you!" she exclaimed. "You're safe!"

Russell breathed a jagged sigh of relief. Cuddled in Blythe's arms was the only place he wanted to be!

As the helicopter lifted into the sky, someone inside it pulled the ladder up, up, up, up until Blythe and Russell were able to hoist themselves inside. Then everyone began to cheer and celebrate!

"How?" Russell asked breathlessly as his friends surrounded him for high fives and hugs. "How did you ever know I was at the top of the Eiffel Tower?"

"It was the lights," Blythe explained. "As soon as they turned on, there was a giant hedgehog-shaped shadow for the entire city to see."

"We put two and two together," Penny Ling continued.

"And zoomed over to pick you up!" Minka finished.

"You guys are the best!" Russell exclaimed, beaming. "Really and truly the best!"

Then his smile faded a little. "I'm so sorry," he began. "About everything! I got so carried away with Project FUN-way that I forgot it was supposed to be fun...for all of us. Can you guys forgive me?"

"Of course!" Blythe said right away as all the pets nodded their heads. "Forgiven... and forgotten."

"Phew!" Russell breathed another sigh of relief. "That's the best news I've heard all day! And speaking of news—guess what, Pepper? I saw Captain Cuddles, and he asked me to tell you hello!"

"Really?" Pepper shrieked happily as her knees went wobbly. Luckily, Blythe was ready to steady Pepper before she toppled over!

Just then, Marc the photographer, who was sitting next to Roger, turned around to talk to Blythe. "I captured the entire rescue! Mona is going to be *thrilled*!" he announced.

"Fantastic!" Blythe said. "Hopefully that means she won't be too angry at us for missing the show."

"Oh, she's not angry at all," Marc replied. "I just texted her to say that we're on our way back. Mona had already decided to switch the order of the event—awards first, fashion show last. So there should be *just* enough time to get everyone onto the runway!"

Blythe's mouth dropped open. "Really?" she squealed. "Project FUN-way is *on*!"

After Roger landed the helicopter, Blythe and the pets sprinted toward the tent. In the darkness, the purple tent shone with brightly colored lights, like a glowing rainbow. Russell had to admit it was more beautiful than he ever could have imagined.

"Hurry, hurry, hurry!" Blythe said anxiously as she rushed to get Russell into his outfit.

"Hey there, sweetheart," Roger said as he touched Blythe's shoulder. "Enjoy this moment—*your* moment. You've earned it."

Blythe pressed her hand over her heart as she smiled at her dad. "Thanks, Dad, you're right. *We've* earned it," she said, gesturing to the pets. Then—suddenly—it was time for Project *FUN*-way to begin!

Zoe pranced onto the catwalk first,

dressed as a doctor in a white coat with rhinestone buttons and a glittering stethoscope around her neck. Next came Minka, wearing a fantastic firefighter outfit that was highlighted with gleaming ribbons. She burst onto the runway between two enormous fireballs—a fabulous special effect that made the crowd gasp!

The lighting suddenly shifted color, casting blue lights against the tinsel backdrop. The tinsel made it seem like everyone was underwater—the perfect effect for Vinnie and Sunil as they marched down the runway in their sea-search uniforms, complete with bright brass buttons.

Red and blue strobe lights flashed as Pepper appeared, dressed as a police officer in a black-and-white uniform with a cool reflective stripe that perfectly comple-mented her fur. Penny Ling came next, wearing a fashion-forward yet functional pilot's uniform. Fans blew at full power as acrobats leaped through the air above her, simulating a rescue scene. The crowd went wild—and Russell realized something. All the unique and unusual ideas his friends had for the show hadn't ruined it.

They'd made it amazing!

"We're up next!" Blythe whispered in Russell's ear. They adjusted their matching search-and-rescue uniforms as they pre-pared to take over the runway. Since Blythe and Russell were the star models from *Tres Blasé*'s best-selling issue, Mona Autumn had insisted that they close the show.

"Let's do it!" Russell said excitedly. Every

single person in the tent burst into wild applause when Blythe and Russell appeared.

Suddenly, Blythe's voice rang through the tent—even though she wasn't speaking.

"Russell! Russell! Hang on, Russell! We're coming!"

Blythe and Russell looked around in confusion. At the same time, they realized what was happening: Mona Autumn was showing the dramatic video footage of Blythe rescuing Russell from the top of the Eiffel Tower! When it was over, the audience's cheers and applause shook the tent!

Mona Autumn strode onto the runway and stood next to Blythe and Russell. "Everyday heroes are everywhere," she announced. "Including our very own Blythe Baxter, who has shown us that *daring* and *dramatic* doesn't just describe today's finest fashions—but the heroes who are always ready to help others!"

It didn't seem possible, but somehow the applause grew even louder. Russell and Blythe beamed, enjoying every moment in the spotlight together. When it was over, they hurried to the VIP area, where their friends were waiting. Soon, they'd be mobbed by well-wishers congratulating them. But for now, the friends simply wanted to celebrate the wild success of Project FUN-way together.

"Tomorrow we'll have to explore Paris *together*. It's a magical city," said Russell. "But for now, let's get to the after-party...I don't know about you, but I am ready for some *fun*!"